Doorbusters

Russell Holbrook

Published by Splatterpiece Press, 2024.

This is a work of fiction. Similarities to real people, places, or events are entirely coincidental.

DOORBUSTERS

First edition. November 8, 2024.

Copyright © 2024 Russell Holbrook.

ISBN: 979-8227089427

Written by Russell Holbrook.

For all retail workers, everywhere.

"Happiness is not in money, but in shopping." - Marilyn Monroe

"The thankful receiver bears a plentiful harvest." - William Blake

Wednesday, Thanksgiving eve

PETE'S JAW CLICKED as he tore another bite of blackened, char-grilled meat from the bone. He turned the meat over in his mouth, smacking loudly, snapping his teeth together and grinding the gristle. A trail of grease trickled from the left corner of his mouth. He glared at the small, flat screen TV that sat atop the mammoth, wood-shell, long-deceased big-box television, staring with contempt at the Black Friday sale commercial parading across the little screen. "It's not right!" He snarled with his mouth full.

Donna glanced up from her plate.

Pete groaned. "These new commercials, they don't have the old magic. I don't understand what happened."

"Maybe the young directors don't have the passion for Black Friday. That's what it seems like to me," Donna offered.

"Yeah, you're right," Pete said. "They don't have the passion, or the respect. They *just don't care*. All they want is a quick buck."

"And the shoppers..." Donna added.

"Ugh! They have no idea! This new generation knows nothing of the Sacred Rite of the Consuming!" Pete swallowed the masticated wad of meat. "They push and shove and brawl and miss all the wonder and the joy."

Donna nodded. "Yes, they miss it all. Poor fools. I actually feel sorry for them."

"Yeah, me too," Pete said.

Donna took another bite of her dinner. Pete shook his head and snagged a sizeable hunk of meat. More grease trickled down his gray stubble-covered double chin.

"Let's not worry about all that right now," Donna said. Her voice soothed him. Pete sighed. "We have this lovely dinner, we have each other, and we still have our special day. No matter how much they try to change it, or wreck it, it's still our day. No one can take that away from us."

She still believes, Pete thought. He offered a pained smile that quickly lost its strength, gave up, and turned upside down. Pete spoke just above a whisper. "I can't stand it, Donna, I just can't. It's so wrong, what they've done, what our day has become. It used to be so pure, so wonderful."

Donna sat her dinner plate on the TV tray standing at her end of the loveseat. A jingle for the season's hot new gaming console blared from the TV. She scooted closer to Pete. "It still can be my love. All the magic, the joy, the excitement; it's still there, we just have to find it."

Her words floated over him. He stopped chewing. Donna's hand slid over Pete's faded navy-blue sweatpants, over the stains of grease, sauce, and cum. Over rips and tears, along the curve of his thigh, her boney fingers glided down and wrapped around Pete's manhood. His scrotum sat neat and warm in the palm of Donna's hand. His hairy, flaccid penis stirred. She cupped him gently.

"Believe," she said.

Pete's eyes glazed over. He whispered, breathlessly, entranced: "Yes."

Donna moved her thin, purple-painted lips closer to Pete's ear. He felt her hot breath against his face. She repeated: "Believe."

Donna's voice sounded far away in Pete's ears. His eyes focused on the TV and what he saw in front of him changed. A soft glow poured out from behind the television. The light grew until it obscured the images on the screen, and then the TV itself was gone, swallowed up as if it were made of light itself. And then, a vision of glory appeared.

Pete saw himself walking with Donna, strolling along the walkway in front of Super Big GigantaMart, arms intertwined, carrying bags overflowing with gift-wrapped items, their faces bright with holiday mirth, their clothes drenched in blood from head to foot, snow falling around them.

"Believe," Donna said, raising her voice.

"Yes," Pete said, his eyes growing wider, his voice stronger. Donna squeezed him. Pete's breath hitched in his throat. "Yes!" He called out.

Then it all became real and Pete saw it because he believed. It was *their* day and no one, not any company or store or commercial could take it from them; not anymore, not ever again. The light blinded Pete and he shut his eyes against it. He felt the front of his sweats coming down and Donna's hot breath on the tip of his shaft, then her lips taking him in and moving up and down. His dinner plate crashed to the carpeted floor. Roaches skittered over his bare feet, rushing to the fallen food. Pete gripped the frayed edges of the loveseat's cushions.

Dancing in the vision behind his closed eyes, Pete saw department store walls dripping with fresh blood. He stood in the center of the store, surrounded by displays of the most coveted gifts of the holiday season. Thunder cracked and register tape poured down from the ceiling. Crimson rain mixed with the falling paper and became a red and white blur. Pete raised his hands and cried out while the torrent of blood and register tape rained down around him.

And then Pete came harder than he could ever remember coming before. His eyes burst open.

Again, he saw the living room and felt the couch beneath him. Donna moved her lips to his. They embraced. Runaway rivulets of semen dripped from their lips as Pete sucked his own cum out of Donna's mouth and their tongues tangled in a lusty rodeo.

Their lips parted and the two lovers gasped for air. Donna fell back on the sunken cushions.

Pete smiled. "My sweet Donna, you always make everything better." Donna smiled back.

"You made me see, baby. You made me see!" Pete said.

"Isn't it beautiful?" Donna said. Pete nodded. Donna smiled, deep and warm. "Wanna finish dinner?" she asked.

"Oh, yeah, I'm even hungrier now than I was before!"

Pete reached down, brushed a crowd of roaches away, and scooped the pile of meat back onto his plate. Donna picked up her piece of bar-b-que and gave it a quick sniff.

"Hey, Pete."

"Yes, dear."

"I think my BBQ here needs some more seasoning. Do you mind?"

Pete smiled. "Oh, no, not at all."

Pete got down on all fours with his sweatpants around his ankles. He bent low and spread his cheeks with both hands to expose his dark, crusty, unwashed anus. Rank fumes filled the air. Donna rubbed the charred, bar-b-qued human foot over Pete's crack and anus and across his hairy, sweat-sparkled taint. After several passes, Donna held the foot under her nose. She inhaled deep. "Mmmmmm... perfect!" She slapped Pete playfully on his left butt cheek. He giggled, stood, and pulled his sweats up.

"Thanks honey," Donna said.

"No problem sweetheart," Pete replied.

And they sat close together and finished their bar-b-que dinner, enjoying each other's company and relishing every bite, knowing that even happier days lay just ahead.

Thursday, Thanksgiving Day

DONNA HELD HER SKINNY arms high. Her bright pink robe cascaded down the length of her lithe frame, brushing against the floor and sending shadows dancing in the candlelight. Magic sparkled in her eyes. "Oh brethren, hear me now! We of the Circle, we who practice the Sacred Rite of the Consuming, on this glorious Black Friday Eve, let us now be united in heart, mind, spirit, and intention!"

A high and frigid wind wound through the drafty old house. The glow of several space heaters burned bright in the background, providing both warmth and soft light. Decaying columns of magazines and newspapers towered in the corners of the great room where the Circle was gathered. Thousands of unopened boxes of electronics lined the baseboards. A mountain of used and discarded dildos and stuffed animals blocked a doorway that led to an outlying room that was crammed to the ceiling with used toilet paper, saved from Donna and Pete's favorite, most memorable bowel movements, the wads of stained paper preserved for eternity in tiny, hermetically sealed glass cases.

Pete and the Eleven sat with legs crossed on the soiled carpet floor, surrounding Donna in a haphazard oval, which was the closest they could get to a circle because of the overwhelming clutter that filled the great room. They raised their pink-robed arms to their Priestess and Donna led them in the sacred chant and together they shouted:

"What's ours for now is ours forever! Shop for now, keep forever!"

With loyal abandon the Circle chanted and felt their spirits soar in strength and unity of purpose. After the thirteenth repetition, the Circle fell silent and waited for their Priestess to speak.

Donna smiled. "Happy Thanksgiving everyone. Let's eat!"

A raucous and jubilant cheer rose from the group as they stood and filed into the dining room.

The Feast

PETE STOOD AT THE HEAD of the long oak table, his trusty electric carving knife in hand. High Priestess Donna stood at the opposite end, handing out the ceremonial pink plastic plates. "Happy Thanksgiving! Be blessed and consume," she said with the passing of each plate, a genuine smile curling her lips.

A massive, homemade aluminum foil platter ran the length of the table. Atop the platter rested the roasted, hog-tied corpse of a voluptuous teenage girl, a rotted apple clenched between her teeth. The horror of the knowledge of unstoppable, impending death was etched into her sewn open, lifeless eyes.

Bobert Wester, an elder of the Circle, was first in line. He leaned in close to the carcass and inhaled deep. He turned and smiled at Pete. "Pete, old boy, the aroma of this roast is positively delectable!"

Pete grinned. "Ah, thanks Bobert! After I injected it in the rump with my personal, special sauce –three loads for the right amount of seasoning- I put 'er in the big roaster out back for the full twelve hours."

Bobert prodded the skin with his pink plastic fork.

"Yep," Pete continued, "Crispy on the outside, moist and chewy on the inside. The trick is to get 'em in there when they're unconscious but still alive, that way the good vibes and energies get trapped in the meat while they cook."

"Ah-ha!" Bobert exclaimed. "You are a master chef indeed!"

"Aw, shucks," Pete said with a shy grin. He waved the electric carving knife over the roast and asked Bobert which cut of meat he'd like to start with. After looking the body over, Bobert pointed at the young woman's posterior.

"Then rump roast it is and rump roast it shall be!" Pete declared in his most regal voice.

He engaged the button, and the knife came alive. While the others chattered away, waiting their turn in line, Bobert drooled and watched Pete maneuver the knife across the girl's plump left ass cheek, carving off a thick, juicy slice of meat and plopping it onto Bobert's outstretched plate.

Bobert smiled, thanked Pete, and moved on to the tray of macaroni and cheese that sat among the myriads of casseroles and side dishes crowding the smaller buffet table that was pushed up against the wall. Donna perked up when she saw Bobert scooping up a hefty spoonful of the gooey concoction.

"Bobert," she called out.

Bobert turned his head as he dumped the food onto his plate. "Yes?"

"I made that mac and cheese from scratch, using the breast milk of this one here," Donna said with a nod to the roasted girl on the platter.

"She was pregnant?" Shirley, a seventh degree Countess of the Couponing, said with an excited gasp.

"She sure was, Shirl. Eight months, at least," Donna replied to her friend. Her eyes widened. "And you know what that means!"

"Veal and baby brain pudding!" The group shouted in unanimous glee.

"Yay! That's right!" Donna said, clapping ecstatically.

Old Pearl, Shirley's great step-aunt, rapped her plastic fork against her plate and shouted, "What a glorious bounty!"

Spurred on by Pearl's words and the wonder of the holiday, everyone cheered and gave thanks.

Smiling from ear-to-ear, Pete winked at Donna. *I love you*, she mouthed silently. *I love you too*, he replied. Feeling overwhelmed with love and gratitude, Pete lowered his knife to the roasted meat and cut in deep.

After the Feast, Black Friday Eve

THE MEMBERS OF THE Circle were huddled together in the living room, reclining on worn-in beanbag chairs, over-sized pillows, and ratty recliners, while Donna and Pete assumed their regal position on the love seat.

The love seat: centerpiece of the room, the location of so many torrid adventures of the flesh. All eyes were glued to the flat-screen TV. While enjoying their desert of baby brain pudding, the Circle watched their traditional holiday favorite, cult director Trevor Kennedy's classic of Christmas carnage, *A Putrid Partridge in a Psychopath's Putamen Part 2: Deck the Halls with Detritus*.

Once the film's final credit had rolled everyone dried their tear-filled eyes with used tissue from Pete and Donna's beloved used tissue collection. When the tears were all wiped away and the tissues were put up for next year, Old Pearl shuffled into the den, removed her ceremonial pink robe, and strapped her kneepads on. Donna followed her. She lit a pillar candle and sat it atop a six-foot-tall stack of ungraded papers that she'd stolen from a first-grade teacher she and Pete had eaten the previous month. Donna loved stealing and collecting ungraded papers from hapless public-school teachers. It was one of her greatest passions.

Watching the large candle warm the room with its soft glow, Donna removed her robe to reveal an eight-inch neon purple strap-on dangling between her legs. She tossed her robe aside and pinched her bare nipples. She took Pearl's hands and looked deep into her eyes.

"Pearl, sweetie, are you ready?" She asked.

Pearl nodded. "Sure thing, darling."

Donna turned and faced the hallway that led to the living room. She shouted, "Pearl hath declared -everybody, get on in here!"

It was time for the Woon Cone, the sacred ritual where all the members of the coven give their love and life energy to the Circle's oldest member in order to harness and focus the power of the group.

Pete and the remainder of the Circle gathered in the small available space near the double-doorway of the den and disrobed. Weaving her hands in the air, Donna whispered an incantation. Pete came forward and handed her a plastic bottle filled with oil that she had harvested from the pimple-riddled faces of a thousand teenage boys. Pearl got down on her hands and knees. Donna poured the oil onto the wizened lady's wrinkled backside, spreading the lube, working it into all her folds and soft, gentle places, like her dusty old puss and her ancient, stained, and shriveled anus.

Donna turned her greasy hands to her fellow believers. "And now let us pour our love into Pearl that she may grow strong and lead us into battle for our righteous cause, to reclaim *our day*!"

"Pearl!" Donna shouted.

"Yes, dear," Pearl answered.

"If thou survive the Woon Cone, dost thou pledgeth to lead thy brethren into righteous battle?"

"Yep, I sure do," Pearl replied.

Donna drew in a deep breath, raising her small breasts high and proud. "Then, by the milk of my husband's loins and the rusty wheel of every shopping cart I hath ever pushed, let the Woon Cone now begin!"

"Woon Cone!" Pete yelped.

"Woon Cone!" The Circle called out together.

And lo, the Woon Cone did begin.

Billy Todd, the youngest member of the circle, eagerly dropped to his knees behind Pearl, his youthful manhood angled high with anticipation. He grabbed onto Pearl's boney hips and with the loose folds of her dusty, thin, wrinkled flesh he—-

Censored!!!!!
(For crude and unnecessary content that in no way helps move the story forward) ...

Censored, again...
And...
Censored some more...

(If anyone thinks that I'm going to explicitly describe a coven of shopping obsessed, mystical cannibals running a train on a sweet old lady, then you're all bonkers! This is a nice story that was made for healthy and wholesome people! So, you'll just have to use your imaginations, which I assume you probably already are. I can see you now, getting all worked up thinking of Old Pearl, slathered with lube, her ancient body getting mercilessly plowed by cocks and dildos alike, being filled with love and passion the likes of which she hadn't felt since her first gangbang behind Jilly's Lo-Lo Mart at the tender yet totally legal age of eighteen, when she first experienced the magic of two-for-one specials and double penetration. And no, I'm not going to tell you about how Old Pearl was so invigorated by the Woon Cone that she went the full three rounds and achieved maximum power and squirted lady juice all over Billy Todd when he was on his third turn. Truly, twas a day that will live in infamy. But, that's enough of that pointless and utterly offensive tangent, let's get on with the story...)

BLACK FRIDAY EVE, CONTINUED...

AFTER THE WOON CONE was completed, Old Pearl sat cross-legged on the floor with the other members surrounding her in a circle. Deep lines of concentration crossed her face. Her eyes moved back and forth behind her closed lids. Everyone in the circle sat in silent meditation.

Several minutes later, a chime sounded in a distant part of the house and the coven opened their eyes. A soft, jaundice-yellow light emanated from Pearl's skin. She smiled and floated up three feet and three inches off the floor. While Pearl levitated, Donna shimmied over to her and held a small golden bowl under the elder's destroyed vagina.

Old Pearl grunted, gave a gentle push, and a perfectly round yellow gumball with a smiley face printed on it slipped out of her and landed in the bowl with a clink. Pearl pushed again, and then again, until thirteen smiley-faced yellow gumballs rested in the golden bowl.

Pearl lowered herself to the floor and took a gumball from the bowl. Donna carried the bowl around the circle with each member of the coven taking a yellow ball. After everyone had one, Donna took a ball for herself.

Donna helped Pearl to her feet and the two stood together in the center of the circle. And Donna declared, "Now, let us take the mystical chew, and rest and dream and grow strong as the hour of our destiny fast approaches."

The coven ate the mystical chews and filed out of the living room with smiles on their faces and wonder in their hearts.

Pete led everyone down to the shed where thirteen custom built plastic storage containers awaited. The warm glow of space heaters filled the old decrepit shed. The coven members quietly slipped into their sleeping bags inside the over-sized containers. Donna and Pete kissed, and each got into their own container. Once everyone was settled, High Priestess Donna addressed the group. With the magic of the mystical chew glowing in her eyes, and with love and reverence she said, "Sleep now, my dears, for the hour of our destiny is nigh!"

And the thirteen members of the coven nestled down in their sleeping bags, closed the lids on their containers, and fell into a deep and tranquil slumber.

Black Friday, 5 A.m. – The Shopping hour

PETE PARKED THE COVEN'S white, unmarked fifteen passenger van in the farthest corner of the Super Big GigantaMart parking lot. One by one, the coven exited the van. A vicious, unseasonably cold wind sliced through the coven members' pink robes but, because of the magic of the mystical chews, the thirteen only felt warmth and joy. Pete and Donna held hands and looked at the train of shoppers that wound from the main entrance down to the far corner and ended in front of the automotive department. They stood hunched and shivering, bundled in their thickest winter clothes, waiting to be let in.

Donna turned to address the coven. "Strap up, everyone; it's time!"

All the coven members, including Pete and Donna, put on their glittering gold fanny packs.

"Now, my dears," Donna hollered, "let's go shopping!"

A cheer went up from the small group and they made their way across the massive parking lot to join the waiting crowd.

5:05 a.m., Inside Super Big GigantaMart

THE EMACIATED WOMAN picked at the oozing scabs on her legs, eating bits of skin and licking globs of yellow-green pus from her unwashed fingers. Several feet away, the store manager and assistant manager paced back and forth.

"Why isn't she in the suit?" The manager asked in a shaky voice. "The doors were supposed to be open five minutes ago, but we can't open until she's in the suit so our beloved mascot, Mr. Mondo-Savo, can greet the crowds!" He fought back the urge to pull at his hair and instead opted for clenching and unclenching his fists.

"She said she won't get in it until Kinsley gets here with her, er... medicine," the assistant manager explained.

The manager leaned in close. "Well, that dammit shit bastard better be here in the next ten minutes or, or... I don't know what, but it won't be good."

"I'm sure he'll be here— oh, look, here he comes," the assistant manager said, pointing to the uniformed employee rushing towards them.

Straining to catch his breath, Kinsley explained, "So, so sorry... there were some... unexpected complications..."

"Kinsley, you assless idgit, I don't give two fucking fucks, just get this bitch in the suit and handle this opening. I'm going to the bathroom to try to move this Thanksgiving dinner. I'll be back in a while," the manager said.

"I'm going out back for a smoke, or three or five. You got this, buddy," the assistant manager added while giving Kinsley a patronizing pat on the shoulder.

Before Kinsley could protest the two men vanished, leaving the hourly employee alone with his would-be mascot. He approached her.

"Destiny?" Kinsley said.

The woman's mouth opened in a three-tooth grin. "Hey, do you got my stuff? I ain't getting' in the suit 'till I get right."

"I do. And I need you to please, please be in uniform and ready to go as soon as possible." He smiled meekly and handed her a small, clear bag filled with clumps of brown crystals.

Destiny eyed the bag suspiciously. "This don't look like my regular, what a what's it?"

Kinsley exhaled hard. "I went to see your guy and he was sold out due to the festive season. So, I went to someone he recommended, a certain Keety Boy, who lives out by the swamp. He sold me this, said it's life changing, and, it's gingerbread flavored."

Destiny's eyes brightened. "Gingerbread meth, what a miracle! I love the holidays! God bless us all and me too!"

"Please, Ms. Destiny, the mascot uniform is in the stock room, along with all the materials you requested for your, um... medicine." Kinsley's eyes seemed to tremble as he spoke.

Destiny smiled and nodded. "Oh yes sir, Mr. Kinsley, I'll be back before you know it!"

The harsh fluorescent lights bore down on Kinsley. His right eye twitched with nerves, and he watched the waifish woman scurry off to the stock room before he turned his sights to the mob just outside the front doors, who were pressed to the glass, eyeing him with contempt. He felt his heart sink. "I hate Black Friday," he muttered to himself as he shuffled out of sight.

Three Minutes and Sixteen Seconds Later

KINSLEY WAS IN THE hardware department, hiding behind a monstrous display of the season's trendiest new chainsaws. He gazed over the pyramid of gas-powered wonders and got lost in his thoughts. *In a few minutes, a horde of burly handymen and super sexy handywomen will be fighting over these,* he brooded. *And those were the same people who picked on me in high school.* He sneered and spit. *I hate them! I hate them and their sexy, successful, handy person ways!!*

Then, as if sent from the Lord above, an idea exploded in Kinsley's mind. Working with the speed and determination only a minimum wage worm can muster, he filled the gas tanks of every chainsaw with the gas and oil mixture cannisters that shared the display with the saws.

Minutes later, with the heavenly fumes swirling in his mind, he yanked a small plastic baggie from his pocket. He hungrily eyed the small brown crystals of gingerbread meth. "I have been up since 2 a.m. I slept 3 hours last night. I couldn't not get some for myself. It's alright; I need this... oh my soul, I truly do need this!"

Kinsley's trembling hands opened the bag. He spilled a clump of the meth onto the lid of a Mr. Weenie winter grill, chopped up a long line with his employee badge and snorted the whole thing in one pull.

Searing heat flared in his nostrils, his eyes bulged and turned red. His hands shook. His cock pulsed and throbbed. He choked and gurgled and fell back. The hair on his palms stood straight up.

"Destiny!" He howled and ran screaming for the stock room.

DESTINY WAS STARING at her legs, watching imaginary neon pink worms and glowing bright, purple maggots weave in and out of the open sores on her legs, when Kinsley stormed through the swinging doors. The bloody needle was still hanging out of Destiny's neck where she'd shot up. The mascot uniform lay draped over a folding chair by her side. "Almost ready, boss," she said when Kinsley burst in.

Kinsley saw a glowing goddess before him. Her matted brown hair was golden silk, her brown and black teeth pearly white, and each oozing sore was a wet vagina, begging to take him inside.

"Destiny!" He howled. "Get ready!"

With their minds synced up by the mysterious drugs, Destiny hiked her soiled skirt to reveal a deep, infected wound on her inner thigh.

"Fill me up, buttercup!" She yipped.

Shouting maniacally, running to her, Kinsley dropped his khaki work pants and buried his two inches of fury in Destiny's flesh, blood and green puss squirting from the hole as he rammed his member into her.

Kinsley screamed, "Oh fuck Destiny, you're so wet!"

Destiny hollered, "Yeah baby, do me like a step child!"

A guttural roar rose up out of Kinsley. His face contorted as he thrust three times and erupted inside Destiny's wound. Stream after stream of cum flowed out of him. His eyes rolled back in his head. His entire body shivered and shook.

Destiny felt the gobs of goo pouring into her, entering her blood stream, coursing through her body. Heat filled her being. Her bowels groaned and shifted. Her muscles bulged. She screamed.

More and more bodily fluids gushed out of Kinsley. His cheeks sunk in and his eyeballs receded as his body deflated.

Destiny's wound suckled on Kinsley's tiny cock, and in moments Kinsley's body was a dried husk. Destiny shoved him off her. He fell to the concrete floor and broke apart into a pile of dust.

Destiny smiled. "Ew yeah, that's what mamma likes." She picked up the mascot costume. "Let's go to work."

After donning the furry blue costume and just before she put on the giant, yellow smiley face head, she fixed up one more, extra-large hit of the gingerbread meth. With a practiced perfection, she injected the drug into the corner of her left eyeball. Then, deep inside her something began to change.

5:27 a.m.

THE COVEN STOOD CLOSE together near the end of the line outside Super Big GigantaMart.

"I wonder what could be taking so long," Pearl said to Donna.

A nearby mammoth, lumbering man overheard Pearl. "I think it's bullshit making us wait out here in the cold like this," he said.

"It's alright, dear, I'm sure we'll be in soon," Pearl replied with a kind hearted grin.

The large man smiled at Pearl. "Hey granny, you're sweet. You got any candy?"

Pearl shared a glance with Donna, then said to the man, "Why, I think I do have some in my purse."

The kindly old mystic drew a round silver tin from her shoulder bag. She twisted off the lid to reveal a mound of little red candies. The man's eyes widened. Pearl held the tin out to him. "Here, take one."

The man's hairy fingers scooped out a candy and quickly popped it in his mouth.

"Mmmmm," he said. "Thanks, granny!"

"You're welcome, dear," Pearl replied.

She turned to a young woman and offered her a candy. The young lady thanked Pearl and accepted. Pearl shuffled through the throng of shoppers, handing out candy from the small tin that seemed to hold an endless supply of the treats. In just a few minutes, she had given a candy to everyone in the line. Upon returning to her friends, she shared a mischievous smile with Donna and put the candy tin back in her purse.

LOOKING OUT AT THE stock room from inside the mascot helmet Destiny felt her world view change. Everything wore a bright, brittle sheen. Tendrils of silver mist, like thin garden snakes, floated out of her nostrils and looped around her until she was surrounded by a great, swirling vortex.

She felt her body morphing, transforming, and binding with the mascot uniform. Her bones snapped and reformed in new configurations. New arms grew from her torso as her two original arms elongated until three seven-foot-long arms danced and swayed from her sides. Her sore-covered legs stretched and took on a spider-like dexterity and appearance.

In the thrall of the change, Destiny wailed in agony, her head burning, melting, and fusing with the huge, bulbous mascot helmet until it was her own head and her face was no longer her face and her body no longer her body for she was transmuted and transmogrified and she was longer her but Destiny had arrived at that which was her namesake and she had become the destroyer, the great beast of Black Friday: Mr. Mondo-Savo!!

"OPEN THE GODDAMM DOOR, you fucks!" The man at the front of the door raged, pounding a closed fist on the glass.

A heavy set woman in dark denim mommy pants pushed forward. "You open this door right this instant; you hear me in there?!"

An irate teenage girl kicked the sliding glass door and screamed something in Spanish, and outrage and impatience spread throughout the crowd.

THE STORE MANAGER ARRIVED back at the front, where the remaining two hourly employees stood observing the mob with growing fright. The manager looked from his employees to the crowd and back again. "Oh brother," he huffed. "Where the goddamm hell are Kinsley and that crack whore who plays Mr. Mondo-Savo??"

"I think they're in the back having sex," Leslie, one of the employees said.

"Yeah, I heard 'um a hootin' and hollerin' back there too," another worker, Ben, added.

The manager, Stafford Brinks, a disgraced former adult film star, merely shook his head and muttered, "God-Mother-Shitting-Dammit ... I guess the three of us will have to deal with the opening by ourselves. Happy Black Friday."

Stafford braced himself, pulled back his shoulders, and with a determined smile, went to open the front doors.

"Wait!" Leslie shouted.

Stafford turned back.

"Leslie... what is it now?"

"Don't let them in, there's something wrong with them!"

"Yeah," Ben added, "they look a might bit looney tunes to me."

"They're just cold, guys, and they want to do their holiday shopping. There's nothing wrong—-"

A sudden barrage of fists bashing the glass doors stilled Stafford's speech. His shoulders hitched. He spun around. The eyes of the shoppers were wide with maniacal rage. The crowd was pressed thick together for as far back as he could see, and from side to side, crammed and smashed and filling the entrance.

"Let us in!" A man screamed.

"Open the fucking doors, you gold brick-shitting corporate pricks!" A millennial woman shrieked.

A toddler screeched unintelligible nonsense and kicked the doors.

The features of the shoppers changed. Their hands grew six times their normal size. Their teeth turned into fangs. Their strength was multiplied by a dozen. The front doors trembled and whined under their wrath. Then they began to chant, a mob choir raising their voices to the sky.

"Let us in! Let us in! Let us in! Let us in!"

DOORBUSTERS

And they pressed in closer and beat upon the doors.

Stafford's face took on a sickly hue. Slowly, he stepped backwards until he'd joined the others.

"Mr. Brinks," Leslie squeaked, "We really, really need to get out of here, like, right now."

A six-year-old girl shrieked and karate chopped the center of the left door, sending a crack rippling up the length of the door. The mob roared.

Stafford Brinks gulped. "Leslie, in case we don't make it out of this, I just want you to know that I've always admired your well-endowed, 22-year-old body, and I've masturbated to fantasies of us together many, many times."

Leslie blushed. "Aww, Mr. Brinks, that's so sweet! You know, I've also pleasured myself more than once or twice while watching your movies."

He beamed. "You've seen my work?"

Leslie grinned seductively while nodding slowly and biting her bottom lip.

Stafford felt a deep stirring within that he hadn't felt in years. "Do you want..."

Leslie nodded and smiled wide.

The manager and the hourly sloth clasped hands and slipped away.

The third employee, Ben, glanced at the mob and then turned and ran after Leslie and Mr. Brinks, calling out, "Hey y'all, wait up!"

"Ever been in a threesome, Ben?" Mr. Brinks asked.

"No, sir, I ain't yet."

Stafford smiled. "My boy, we'll make a cocksmith out of you yet!"

A minute later, the three employees took refuge in Stafford Brinks' office to hide away from the ever-encroaching terror.

Seventy-three seconds later, Mr. Brinks was thrown out of his own office due to poor job performance.

"Get the fuck out!" Leslie screamed. "You didn't even last thirty seconds inside me! I guess it's true what they say, 'Never have spontaneous three-ways with your heroes.'"

Pantsless, scared, and demoralized, Stafford Brinks stood outside his office and listened to the moans and demands of Leslie as her nubile flesh was relentlessly pounded by a hillbilly stock boy.

Something soft and fuzzy tickled his bare butt cheeks, startling Stafford out of his self-pity. "Hey, what the—"

A furry blue hand rammed up his anus, splitting him open. The hand and arm pushed deep into him, lifted, and spun him around until the manager was face to face with the Mr. Mondo-Savo abomination. He howled. Tears flowed down his burning, flushed red cheeks.

Mr. Mondo-Savo hurled the manager against the office door. Stafford's head smashed through the cheap, fake wood, startling Leslie and Jarret, who went into a frenzy of speed humping and shrieking.

The mascot rammed Stafford's body into the door over and over, breaking it down bit by bit.

AN ENRAGED MIDDLE-AGED housewife smashed her fist through the glass, ripping the flesh from her hand. She seemed not to notice as she reared back and put it through again, breaking off more of the glass and tearing off more 9d her hand. The throng of maniacs behind her pressed in harder. The doors moaned and bowed under the strain, sending more cracks scattering over the steadily disintegrating surface.

THE COVEN STOOD BACK and watched the wild mass of shoppers pushing and shoving and smashing together.

Pete's eyes sparkled with glee.

The door's metal frame faltered.

A chorus of shattering glass rang out into the early morning sky.

DOORBUSTERS

JUST AS LESLIE AND Jarret were experiencing the most intense orgasm of their lives, what remained of the office door exploded inward. Mr. Mondo-Savo roared and stormed into the room and began beating the young couple with the puppet corpse of their dead manager.

THE HORDE OF IRATE shoppers plowed through the front doors, breaking the metal frame, spreading broken glass over the entirety of the entrance. They barked and howled and fought, knocking over displays, desperately trying to take any treasured item that another shopper had.

PETE AND DONNA LED the coven into the store, strolling casually, observing the chaos in front of them. Donna patted Pearl on the shoulder. "My goodness, Pearl, those special candies of yours sure did the job."

Pearl smiled and giggled. "Yep, they always do!"

The two mystics laughed as the coven ventured into the store.

HEARING THE COMMOTION at the front of the store, Mr. Mondo-Savo piled Stafford Brinks' dead body onto the corpses of his two employees and hurried to see what was happening. With his six fuzzy arms dancing, the mutated mascot ran into the store.

A tween boy with braces and a lisp recognized the mascot and called out to him. Mr. Mondo-Savo snatched up the boy and tossed him into the air. The boy sailed across the mammoth store and crashed down in housewares, snapping his neck on a shelf. Mr. Mondo-Savo danced and twirled between racks and down isles until he did a triple-whirl and found himself in front of the pyramid chainsaw display. His heart soared with glee. He laughed triumphantly and, one by one, he began to fire up the saws.

A RUMBLE CAME FROM above, causing the high ceiling to shiver. Mist crawled over the rafters from an unseen source. Donna looked at Pearl. The old lady shook her head. "I don't know what it is, dear, I'm not the one doing it."

Donna's mouth fell open. Her wide eyes met Pete's. They clasped hands. Pearl took Donna's hand. Bobert took Pearl's hand, and the entire coven linked hands and formed a circle, all of them feeling the supernatural stirrings around them.

WHEN THE BURLY HANDYMEN and the sexy handywomen saw Mr. Mondo-Savo with the chainsaws, the new and shiny ones they knew they were meant to have, jealousy and hatred filled their hearts and a new surge of rage rose within them.

"Hey Mr. Mondo-Savo!" A man in trendy outdoorsy work clothes shouted, "Those are our chainsaws, you can't have them!"

A super sexy landscaping lady screamed, "You don't deserve a chainsaw! You're not a handyperson, you're just a stupid mascot!"

Mr. Mondo-Savo gasped. His arms stopped dancing. The mirth fell from his round, yellow face. He leveled his solid black eyes at the landscaping lady. Thirty-six chainsaws sat idling, scattered around on the display and on the floor. A low, seething sound crept out of the mascot's dead mouth and grew louder, mingling with the chainsaw motors and rising above them.

The ceiling rumbled and shook. Mr. Mondo-Savo snatched up six chainsaws, one in each hand, and spun toward the mob of handymen and women marching toward him. The renowned holiday song, "Flight of the Sugarplum Nut Blasters", erupted out of the store's overhead speakers that pumped out the sickening seasonal tunes every year.

Six chainsaws buzzed, cutting through fabric and flesh. The mascot sliced off the trendy man's legs as he tried to run by. He sawed off the landscaping lady's face. He cut an aspiring teen handyperson in half.

Leon LaLouche, local tree destroyer, rushed Mr. Mondo-Savo with a chainsaw in each hand. He swung, severing one of the mascot's left arms. The severed arm flew through the air on its own, as if being controlled telepathically by the mascot, and buried the chainsaw's blade in Leon's mouth, pushing all the way through and out the back of his bald head, and pulling up and through his brain and then swinging and sawing and removing the man's head in three cuts.

The remaining chainsaw enthusiasts encircled Mr. Mondo-Savo, each with a blaring saw in their trembling hands. They let out a fierce battle cry.

Thunder crashed above.

The fluorescent lights exploded.

Darkness and mist filled the store.

Emergency lights flashed on.

The shoppers roared and hurled themselves into battle. Like a ballerina with magic wings, Mr. Mondo-Savo twirled in his soiled pink slip-on shoes. Blades spun, clashed, and whined. Sparks danced. Severed limbs fell to the floor. Blood spewed and gushed. Bodies and parts of bodies crashed down on the concrete floor and Mr. Mondo-Savo articulated the massacre with beautiful precision.

ACROSS THE STORE, THE coven held hands and listened to the roaring chainsaws and the screaming shoppers. Their minds synced and above them, the mist began to swirl.

SHOPPERS RAN THROUGH Super Big GigantaMart filling carts with the precious consumer bounty. In electronics, an enraged step-uncle fought furiously with two teens who were trying to take the last Judith Sonnets Greatest Hits home recording console.

In kitchen supplies, a celebrated local fry cook bashed in his boyfriend's face with a meat tenderizer. In sporting goods, the high school ROTC members were loading rifles and shotguns that they had been coveting all year, but their parents had refused to buy them. But now their parents were dead because the ROTC children had bashed in their brains with the shiny new golf clubs that their fathers loved more than their children and no one would ever refuse them anything else ever again. With loaded weapons in their hands and hate in their minds they filed out into the store.

And the hatred and rage and the love of *things* and the want for those things to somehow give their lives meaning poured out of the shoppers and filled the gargantuan department store, rising to the ceiling, palpable, taking physical form in the mist. Lightning danced overhead, thunder cracked, and a storm began to rage.

THE COVEN FELT THE malignant energy of the mob. They closed their eyes and concentrated. A gust of wind whipped through the store. More thunder crashed. Out of the mist, black clouds formed and slowly began to swirl, creating a vortex above them.

Suddenly, Pearl broke from the circle. She raised her hands and pointed at the dark, swirling mass in the ceiling. "Children, help me!" She shouted.

A nearby shopper with a cart full of appliances screamed at them, "You freaks! You're doing this! You're trying to ruin the best Black Friday ever!"

"No!" Pete shouted back. "We love Black Friday; we're trying to save it!"

The wind howled, louder, stronger, and the roar of chainsaws grew closer.

Blood and skin and viscera flew as Mr. Mondo-Savo sawed his way through the men's clothing section, draping spleens and intestines over the sales racks of jeans and slacks.

At the edge of the footwear aisle, the coven trembled.

"Alas, he is headed straight for us!" Bobert shrieked into the wind.

"Concentrate, children!" Pearl commanded.

While Mr. Mondo-Savo gutted an overweight man with a cart full of feminine hygiene products, the coven focused all their power on the vortex above.

The vortex spun faster and faster and faster and faster, pulling into itself, until a rip in the dimensional fabric appeared, first a tiny tear, and then growing and growing, gaining strength, and creating its own gravitational pull.

"Push!" Pearl commanded, stepping out, focusing on the vortex. Her eyes burned bright white. She began reciting the sacred words of the emergency incantation that can only be used in the direst of shopping emergencies.

"It's the magic of the Woon Cone!" Pete yelled. "Pearl's using it!"

From every corner of the store, every shopper pushed their overflowing carts to the center of Super Big GigantaMart, gathering beneath the vortex.

The ROTC team stepped out of the snack aisle, raised their guns, and fired into the crowd. Shoppers caught bullets to the face. Heads exploded. Chests burst. The shooters grinned.

Mr. Mondo-Savo leapt from the shadows and swung his saws wildly at the boys. His severed, flying arm came in close behind and decapitated a random elderly man who had just cleaned out the pharmacy's supply of Titanium Dick Erectors, then gutted two of the boys before they could angle their rifles on him.

The vortex swirled faster and faster! The coven focused all their power and, with unified intention, filled the spinning clouds with the gale force of ten category five hurricanes combined with the strength of a drunk black hole cosmic collapse. And like metal shavings to a magnet, or loose high school girls to a BOGO sale on morning after pills, the hundreds of shoppers filling the store were pulled toward the vortex portal thingy.

Purple lightning flashed in the mist and fog surrounded the portal.

"Pearl! What's happening?" Billy Todd shouted.

"Our magic has combined with some dark swamp juju that someone brought into our sphere, and the clash of energies caused a tear in the veil between dimensions, which opened that portal thingy up there," Pearl explained, nodding to the swirling mass above.

"Awesome!" Billy Todd yelped. He raised his hands higher and felt the power pouring out of him. "So, what are we doing?"

Pearl's eyes darted back and forth. "We're... um... helping?"

"Why?"

Pearl shrugged. "I'm not totally sure. It was an intuitive decision. I'm just going with it."

"Intuitive! Sweeeettt!" Billy Todd shouted.

A MASS OF SCREECHING, shouting, and whining voices filled the air as the hordes of Black Friday patrons drew near.

A woman and man, each clutching the handlebar of a scooter and cursing at one another, were yanked off the floor and sucked into the vortex portal thingy. The portal grumbled with satisfaction and grew stronger, plucking shopper after shopper up into itself, inhaling carts brimming over with items along with them.

The ROTC team shot at the vortex, but it sucked away their guns and pulled them in along with the shelves that they clung to.

More and more shoppers and merchandise disappeared into the giant swirling mass. Black storm clouds formed and stretched across the ceiling for the entire length and width of the store. An indignant peal of thunder shook the building to its foundation and blood rained down from the clouds.

The roaring winds carried the searing buzz of chainsaws to the coven members' ears.

Pete pointed and shouted, "Look, there!"

The eyes of the coven collectively turned and saw Mr. Mondo-Savo hopping across the shelf tops. His severed arm flew ahead like a guide in a storm, buzzing, disemboweling, and decapitating shoppers who were hurling towards the vortex portal. Then, like a master butcher, he leapt into the flowing stream of flying shoppers who still clung to their precious packages and boxes and merchandise. The abominable mascot from hell danced so with his spinning blades that all the cuts he made were deadly and severe, and all shoppers far and near, could not escape the saw on the swinging fuzzy paw that sliced and diced and maimed and brought infernal fame to the glorious one who came with gingerbread meth in his veins twas no who was safe, oh, from the wrath of Mr. Mondo-Savo!

The hell-spawned mascot flew into the last cluster of shoppers, a group of prostitution enthusiasts and semi-professional machine gun polishers. He rammed into them and shoved a spinning blade deep inside each one of them.

"Now you know how it feels to have something big and unwanted inside of you!" A tiny, angry, feminine voice squeaked from beneath the mascot head. It was Destiny. She was still there. She mustered all her meth strength, and her soul became one with the spirit of Mr. Mondo-Savo. She rose her voice and shouted, "Now, let's go home; I still haven't had my Thanksgiving dinner!"

And with a burst of methamphetamine speed and energy, Mr. Mondo-Savo, and the Destiny inside, flew into the vortex portal thingy, taking the last cluster of shoppers and a mass of stray body parts with them.

A deep rumble came from the vortex. Lightning pulsed and flashed and crashed back and forth overhead. The portal let out an ear-splitting groan.

The coven covered their ears and shrieked in pain. A tsunami of blood, bile, viscera, and partially digested body parts exploded from the vortex portal thingy.

The vile wave crashed down on the coven and swept them away. Through housewares, past electronics, over the self-check-out aisles, and out the destroyed front entrance where a fresh new blanket of snow broke their fall.

The wave of blood and gore subsided, and the members of the Circle slowly got to their feet, checking each other to make sure everyone was okay and accounted for. The snow fell heavy and stuck to their blood-soaked robes.

Pete helped Donna up. They held each other and gazed at the snow in wonder. "It's like... it's like the..." Pete faltered.

Donna smiled. "I know."

Tears welled in Pete's eyes. "It's so beautiful!"

Donna nodded and brought her beloved husband in for a kiss.

A pair of squeaking wheels caught the coven's attention, for they knew there was only one kind of wheel that made that sound, the cart of an extra-sized Super Big Giganta-Cart with worn out wheels desperately in need of oiling.

"Grandma Pearl!" A cheery voice called out.

"Brenden!" Pearl responded, smiling at the young man. "There you are, and right on time, too!"

Brenden, the Super Big GigantaMart assistant manager, walked gingerly through the falling snow, pushing a cart piled high with shiny, wrapped gifts of every sort.

Donna's mouth fell open. "What's this, Pearl?"

Pearl smiled and mischief lit up her eyes.

"I know what it is," Pete interjected, "It's the Black Friday magic!"

"Sweeeeettt Black Friday magic!" Billy Todd yipped while thrusting his hips.

"And, it helps to have someone on the inside," Pearl said.

Donna let out a hearty laugh. "Oh Pearl, you fantastic old coot!" She turned to address the coven. "Come on everybody, let's go home, get cleaned up, and have leftovers!"

A cheer of approval went through the group of friends and they began stepping off the walkway and into the parking lot to begin the long trek back to the van.

Pete's heart overflowed with cheer. "God bless us all!" He shouted.

"...And me too!" An angry voice screamed from behind them.

Six chainsaws roared. Mr. Mondo-Savo flew out the front doors. And screams of horror echoed through the snowy Black Friday morning.

The End?

DONNA'S BABY BRAIN Pudding

Ingredients

Brains of one fresh infant, preferably 7 to 9 months of age (the fresher the better!)

2 cups powdered sugar

One 16 oz. can of extra heavy cream

4 teaspoons imitation vanilla extract

4 teaspoons cinnamon

3 grams cocaine

1 teaspoon nutmeg

Pinch of salt

Preparation

Pulse the baby brains, cream, and vanilla in a blender until you get a gooey, mushy, but still lumpy consistency. Transfer to a large mixing bowl and stir in the dry ingredients. Once everything is well combined, transfer to a heavily oiled (baby lard works best!) baking dish and bake at 400 degrees for 33 minutes or until the top is golden brown. Then, enjoy warm with friends and family!

"Night of the Wereclown"

Tuesday, December 22nd
1:45 a.m.
Persuader's Lounge
Mable Town, USA

"Last call!" Leryl the bartender hollered over the din of the rowdy holiday crowd.

Basil shouted to Merry, "Should we get one more drink?"

Before the question was complete, Merry was already bounding towards the bar, leaving Basil watching her weave through the crowd with a smile on his face. He chuckled and hurried after her.

After two pints of draft ale had been served to a towering, bearded man in a Santa suit, Basil and Merry pressed up against the bar.

"Two more Blitzen specials, please Leryl!" Merry called out.

Leryl the bartender nodded and poured the drinks. A moment later the young couple were sipping their booze and settling their tab. The crowd thinned, the noise level subsided, and Leryl made small talk with his two favorite regulars.

"You kids need me to call you a ride," Leryl asked Basil.

Basil waved him away. " Nah, we're on foot. Thanks, though."

"You're the best, Leryl! If I didn't love this fucker here," Merry said, playfully jabbing Basil in the ribs with a skinny elbow, "I'd ride your mustache from here to Sunday morning."

Leryl grinned. "Too bad I don't have a mustache."

"It's a tragedy. You could totally rock a 'stache!" she said.

They all three broke into a fit of laughter that ended simultaneously with the last song on the jukebox. Leryl's mouth turned down. "Listen, you kids be careful walking home tonight. It's the fourth Tuesday of the month. It's not exactly safe."

"Aw, don't worry, Leryl, we'll be fine," Merry said.

"Which way are you two going?"

"We always cut through the park, then along the town square to our apartment," Basil explained.

Leryl's brow tightened. "You two still live in Lamplighter Village?"

Merry and Basil nodded.

Leryl sighed. "The park? Really?"

"The hilly rolls of grass are all covered in the fog this time of year; it's so pretty," Merry said wistfully.

Leryl nodded in agreement, then added, "Just promise me you'll stay on the path, alright?"

Merry and Basil smiled and giggled. "Sure thing, Leryl," Basil said.

Leryl slammed his fist down on the bar. "Goddammit! This is serious!"

The young couple started at the bartender's outburst.

"I'm sorry," Leryl huffed, "but you two need to know that there's dangerous things that lurk in the pretty winter fog and I... I... " His voice caught in his throat. He sniffled. "...I just want you guys to get home safe."

Merry's face went slack. "Oh no Leryl, it's okay, it's okay. What's this all about?"

"Yeah, buddy, why are you getting so upset?" Basil asked.

Leryl's eyes darted around. He watched the huge Santa man stumble out the door into the cold, misty night. "Okay, if I give you guys another round or two on the house, will you hang around and let me tell you a story?"

"We love stories, man, you don't have to bribe us with drinks!" Basil said. "But free drinks are always appreciated."

"Alright then, I'll tell you everything."

Leryl left the bar, locked the front door, and returned to fix his favorite couple two more Blitzen specials. As he poured and mixed the drinks, he began. "It happened exactly one year ago, on a cold, foggy winter night. Two young lovers were walking through Mable Birch Park, on their way home from the bar..."

"THIS FOG IS REALLY something," Dylan said.

Lauren, Dylan's fiancé, squeezed his arm and pulled in close. "I think it's beautiful. Look at the way it's hovering over the hilly rolls of grass."

"Yeah, it is nice," Dylan mused.

The young couple strolled along the path, the pit-pat of their feet on the pavement the only sound in the still, winter night.

"I love the park at night," Lauren said.

Dylan glanced at his watch. "Technically, it's early morning."

"What time is it?"

"It's five minutes after three. We left Persuader's just before two."

"Wow, we have been wandering around for a while."

A mischievous smile crossed Lauren's lips. She said, "We're almost to the playground."

Dylan caught the glint in her eyes. He grinned. "Oh, are we?"

Lauren nodded. "And the fog is so romantic, and it's our old spot."

"From back before we had a warm bed in a well-heated apartment, you mean." Dylan chuckled.

"But it's our spot, on the squishy mat under the magic castle fort."

"It was definitely magic."

"Oh baby, please, just for a little while. I need the touch," Lauren purred and batted her long, black eyelashes.

Dylan's drunk, glassy eyes met Lauren's. "Okay, you convinced me."

Lauren let out a quiet squeal and they left the path and made their way through the thick fog to their old spot underneath the magic castle play fort, the place they'd spent so many secret nights as teenagers, exploring each other's bodies in the pale moonlight. But there was no moonlight, and the off the path, the park was cloaked in thick darkness. After struggling to find magic castle and crawling into their hidden place, the gloom swallowed them up. Bumping into each other and laughing, they fought with their clothes until they were naked and holding each other close to fend off the cold. They pressed their bodies together and joined their flesh.

Merry gasped. Basil groaned. Someone outside the castle cackled.

"What was that noise, that voice?" Basil said.

Merry dug her nails into his backside and bucked her hips. "Who cares, just give it to me. Gimme the touch!"

"Okay, okay!" Basil said.

Basil placed his thumb on Merry's forehead and his tongue in her ear. She squealed and raked jagged red lines along Basil's back. He thrust harder. He moaned into his lover's ear. Maniacal cackles echoed through the fog.

"Merry! There it is again!" Basil whisper-shouted.

"Dylan, why'd you call me 'Merry'?"

"I'm not Dylan! It's me, Basil!"

"Oh no, Ohio! I'm not Lauren, I'm Merry!" Merry said, grabbing Basil and bouncing under him.

Basil's eyes blared panic. "We're the ones in the story, not Dylan and Lauren! There is no Dylan and Lauren; it's us! What the hell was in those drinks??"

Merry cackled loudly beneath Basil. "Mostly clown blood and a splash of Grenadine! And that wasn't a story!"

Basil looked down at Merry. Her skin was pasty pancake white. Thick black rings swarmed around her wide insane eyes. Pearl white fangs glistened under bright red lips. Her beautiful, natural brown hair was a neon blue mess.

Basil screamed. Merry howled with laughter and sunk her hungry fangs deep into Basil's neck. She dug her nails deep in his back and moved her hips while she held him in place. Basil's body shook as he erupted inside her while she ravaged his veins, draining Basil of his blood.

Merry felt Basil go limp inside her. She flipped him onto his back. Straddling him and holding his mouth open wide, she shoved her fingers down her throat and gagged herself. Bright red cotton candy streamed from Merry's mouth down into Basil's parted lips. Merry worked the cotton candy deep into her barely conscious lover's mouth, and he began to chew, hesitantly at first, like an automatic response to keep from choking, then with gusto, moaning with satisfaction until he whimpered softly and passed out.

DOORBUSTERS

Exactly 13 Seconds Later

Basil's eyes shot wide open and grew to twice their usual size, bulging and bleeding at the edges. His body seized. He shrieked in disharmonic tri-tones. Tears rolled down his bulbous cheeks. His tongue turned black. His skin washed the palest white, as if his entire naked body had been painted with make-up. Cherry red covered his cracked lips.

His light blonde hair was pushed out by a mane of thick, bright green scraggle. His muscles rippled and swelled. All his teeth turned into sharp, pointed fangs and his fingernails grew into bitter knives. And his mind swirled with dreams of horror and destruction.

Next to Basil, his clothes shape-shifted into a ridiculous, neon yellow clown costume.

The pain and shock of the transformation subsided, and Basil lay still, catching his breath, recognizing his surroundings, the realization of his Becoming gradually dawning on him. He took in a deep breath and began to giggle. Then, he heard Merry's voice next to him, laughing along with him. And joining their voices Basil heard a crowd of giggles and laughs surrounding the playground. As he laughed, his clown clothes and giant wacky shoes slithered onto his body.

Now dressed in her own clown outfit, Merry laid down next to Basil. They clasped hands and slid out of the play fort, giggling hysterically. Out in the center of the playground, they popped straight up.

Clown after chuckling clown stepped out of the dense fog until Merry and Basil were encircled. They wore painted smiles and bright colorful costumes that were soaked in blood.

A clown with strings of intestines draped around her neck stepped forward to Basil. Taking one of the loops from her neck, she blew into it. The intestine expanded and the clown twisted and pulled at it and formed it into the shape of a giraffe. The clown smiled and shyly held the intestine animal out to Basil.

"Aww, look honey, Woozy made you an intestine animal! That's so sweet!" Merry said.

Basil took the animal and smiled. He looked at the clowns around him.

Merry squeezed his hand. "You're a wereclown now. This is your family."

"Why did you turn me?"

"Are you mad that I did?"

Basil looked at his oversized clown hands with their razor-sharp nails and his big floppy orange shoes. "No way; this is awesome!"

"Whew! I'm so glad to hear you say that! I wanted us to live together forever, and now we can!"

"Wereclowns are immortal?"

Merry grinned. "Among other things."

A murmur of laughter rippled through the gathered clowns.

"There's so much for you to learn, darling," Merry said in a voice that was both sweet and sultry. Basil felt a strong stirring in his clown trousers. "But for now, we need to get you something to drink."

"I am kinda parched," Basil said with a shrug.

"Follow Woozy. We'll travel in the fog," Merry said.

Woozy motioned them towards the fog and Marry and Basil followed.

MERRY DRAINED THE LAST of her drink and sat her glass on the bar. She placed her hands on the bar to steady herself. "Wow, that last one was extra strength, Leryl."

"And that was a great story too," Basil added. He swayed on his stool and giggled. "I like how you changed the names to be like, our names."

"Yeah, Leryl, tha - that was cool how you did that," Merry said.

Leryl smiled warmly. "Thanks guys, I'm really glad you enjoyed it."

Merry and Basil grunted and giggled. Leryl grinned and chuckled and said, "I love stories."

The low laughter and fits of giggles infected all three of them. The sounds of mirth filled the room. Laughter seemed to echo from the very walls themselves.

Clutching his side, and with tears streaming down his cheeks, Basil asked, "Hey Leryl, what's in a Blitzen special anyway?"

"Mostly clown blood, with a splash of Grenadine!" Leryl replied with a laugh.

"But just a splash!" Merry howled.

"That's right! That's all it takes!" Leryl roared, opening his mouth wide to reveal rows of glistening white, pointed fangs.

The End

And now, an unedited excerpt from the forthcoming

Meth Alley Massacre

Coming Christmas 2025!!

Christmas Eve
Mable Town

Keety Boy swung the chainsaw. The jagged teeth dug into the old woman's head.

Blood sprayed up to the nicotine-stained ceiling of the double-wide trailer. Bits of flesh and bone and splashes of crimson coated Keety Boy's face, hands, and ugly Christmas sweater. He pushed down harder. His knuckles went white. He screamed.

The saw blade finished its diagonal trek through Mawmaw's head and the left side of her face and skull slid off. Keety Boy fell forward with the momentum and the weight of the gurgling chainsaw. His blubbery body bumped into Mawmaw's tiny four-foot-three frame. She glared at her grandson through her one remaining eye.

Mawmaw shoved Keety Boy. He flew across the room, smashing into the Christmas tree and collapsing in a tangled pile of colorful lights and glistening garland.

The chainsaw clattered away, sputtered, and died. Keety Boy rolled off the fallen tree and reached for the saw.

"Goddammit Mawmaw, it's Christmas!" He screeched. "And you done rurnt the tree!"

Garbled sounds and a trail of black saliva oozed from the old crone's mouth. She coughed and a stream of slugs flowed over her tongue and spilled down her chin. Her remaining eye flashed bright green and red in a slow strobing pattern. "Ain't no presents for Chrisssmass this year," she hissed.

Keety Boy's eyes twisted up. "What?"

Mawmaw's feet left the floor. Holding out her arms, she floated toward her grandson, her one eye flashing, blood running down her face and neck.

"*Silent night, holy night, all is calm, all is bright,*" Mawmaw sang in a watery cadence. More black bile poured from her mouth. She let out a deep, wet chuckle. "Come to Mawmaw now, boy."

Keety Boy scrambled to his feet and yanked the chainsaw's cord. The engine revved and died.

"Goddammit, please help me, lord Jesus!"

He jerked the cord again. The engine screamed with life. Tears formed in Keety Boy's eyes.

Three Days Earlier

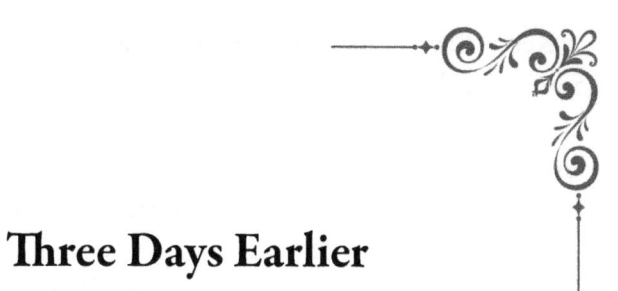

Christmas Eve, Eve, Eve
9:42 p.m.

Keety Boy stretched out his pasty arms and proclaimed, "This is gonna be the best goddamned Christmas ever!"

His eyes were bright, his smile was wide; he was high out of his ever-loving mind.

Mawmaw, the family's minuscule matriarch, padded into the living room of the double-wide trailer that she shared with her husband, her grandson, and a constantly rotating gang of family members needing or wanting a place to stay and come down off whatever drug they were binging on at the moment, or to do more of whatever drug it might be. She shot a look at Keety Boy, her beady eyes squinting. "Wha chu hollerin' about there, boy?"

"Christmas, Mawmaw! I'm hollerin' about Christmas!" Keety Boy shouted.

The withered grandmother peered out from the scraggly white and nicotine stained mane that surrounded and nearly obscured her tan, wrinkled face. "What about it?"

"It's gonna be the best one ever, ever, ever!" Keety Boy said, his voice booming throughout the trailer.

Mawmaw winced at the volume of her grandson's holiday cheer.

The rickety master bedroom door squeaked open and Pawpaw stumbled out wearing nothing but his favorite pair of urine stained tighty-whities. He looked at his grandson with a wrinkled, questioning brow.

"I'M HOLLERIN' ABOUT Christmas, Pawpaw!" Keety Boy shouted. He thrust a tangled bundle of Christmas lights at his grandfather.

Pawpaw took the multi-colored lights from Keety Boy. He smiled, scratched his beer belly, and glanced at the unadorned artificial tree that leaned in the corner of the living room.

"C'mon, Pawpaw, the lights go on first," Keety Boy said, his face aglow with holiday cheer and high-powered homemade narcotics.

Pawpaw yawned and raised his eyebrows.

Keety Boy nodded toward the coffee table in front of the couch. A massive droplet of sweat dangled precariously from the tip of his nose.

Pawpaw stumbled over to the table and picked up the Shorty Trickum Cuntry Christmas commemorative plate, shoved the accompanying communal short pink straw into his left nostril, and snorted one of the six rails of meth that were lined up across the ceramic surface. After inhaling the powder, Pawpaw sat the plate back down, blinked his eyes rapidly, and then blurted out something unintelligible in backwards Spanish.

"I know that's right!" Keety Boy said laughing, his belly jiggling underneath his ugly Christmas sweater. He looked at Pawpaw with teary, affectionate eyes as the elder of the family enthusiastically scratched his ass.

No one was quite sure where Pawpaw had come from. Thirty years earlier he'd ambled up through the borderlands. Mawmaw had picked him up at her favorite bar, Persuader's, and brought him back to her double-wide den of iniquity in the third-to-last trailer on the left on Meth Alley, the most notorious street in Mable Town.

Back then, Pawpaw was a wily young thing with dreams of curly fries and strip mall shopping abandon. Mawmaw was a spell-wielding-swamp-mama-turned-townie twice his age, determined to tame him with her witchy sex powers, and instruct him in the ways of gas station gambling.

As it had been ordained by the Fates, their love grew and they were married three hours and thirteen minutes later, beside a dumpster behind the bar, while a derelict step-uncle known by the name of Pamela looked on and masturbated in the bushes.

The children of the double-wide each had a different father whom they had only met through Mawmaw's liquor fueled reminiscences. As a result, the five children, overjoyed at the possibility of a dad, of one who would stay and love them, immediately clung to the new young man, who incidentally was only a few years older than they were which made him that much more relatable.

Some years passed and the children accidentally spawned children of their own. The stepfather, who had by then grown a proud and enviable mustache, became much beloved by the grandchildren and was appointed the time honored Southern American title of "Pawpaw". This worked out well, for everyone had forgotten his original name years ago.

Mawmaw sat on the couch, snorted a rail of Keety Boy's homemade meth, and lit a cigarette. Exhaling, she felt the familiar surge in her veins. "This here's a good batch, Keety."

"Thanks, Mawmaw!" Keety Boy said, furiously pulling a length of golden garland from a box. "You just wait 'till you try my special Christmas batch that I'm gonna be cookin' up here real soon."

Mawmaw smiled. "I'm sure it'll be great." She snorted and spit. "Where'd you get the recipe?"

"For this batch I got the recipe from *Meth Method 101 Cookbook*, but my next one'll be a special Christmas flavor," Keety Boy said.

"Where'd you get that'n from, the Chrismass flavor?"

"Ain't found it yet, just got an idea."

Just then Pawpaw found his hands wound in tangled strings of Christmas tree lights. He blurted out another curse in Spanish. Keety Boy gasped. "No, Pawpaw, that ain't how they go." He reached over. "Here, lemme help you with that."

Keety Boy began to carefully untangle the lights from Pawpaw's hands and wrists.

"You gotta be careful where you get them Christmas recipes from now," Mawmaw said.

Keety Boy nodded. "Uh huh, sure Mawmaw."

Pawpaw giggled and tugged at the strings of lights. "Stay still, let me get 'em," Keety Boy said to him.

"And whatever you do, don't you go messin' with my *Christmas Cauldron* Cookbook. Them recipes there got enchantments, things you young don't know nothin' about. Keep a mind, don't you go near it," Mawmaw said.

Keety Boy struggled with the tangled strings of lights, slowly freeing them up a bit at a time. Mawmaw squinted at him.

"You hear me, boy?" She asked.

"Yeah Maw, Maw, I hear you," he said, his eyes focused on his work.

"Alright then, just so's you know," Mawmaw said before she lit another cigarette.

Keety Boy pulled the last remaining knot and the final tangle came free. "Ya-yuh!" He cried in triumph.

Pawpaw smiled and began to wind the lights through the branches of the Christmas tree. Keety Boy joined him without a thought of a word that Mawmaw had said.

Seventeen and three-quarter minutes later the leaning tree of twinkly joy was lit, adorned, and weighted down with every available ornament and trinket that Pawpaw and Keety Boy could scavenge from the clutter of the storage closet.

Keety Boy, Mawmaw, and Pawpaw sat on the couch together, tweaking and twitching and soaking in the sparkling wonder of the tree.

"It's so beautiful," Keety Boy whispered in awe.

Mawmaw mumbled an agreement.

Pawpaw leaned over the edge of the sofa and threw up. He sat back and wiped his lips with the back of his hand and mumbled backwards phrases that only he could hear, personal prophecies which filled him with a nameless dread.

Keety Boy beamed with joy. The lights on the tree twinkled and reflected in his glazed, glassy eyes. He whispered to himself, "It's gone be the best Christmas ever. Bester than ever, ever. I just know it." And a single, joyful tear rolled down his cheek.

Two Days Earlier

Christmas Eve, Eve

DOORBUSTERS

Keety Boy was cutting up a rail of meth when Rosie burst through the trailer's front floor, startling Keety and causing him to almost spill his drugs.

"Wassup, nigga?" Rosie shouted.

Keety Boy cringed at Rosie's use of the N-Word.

"Rosie!" He shouted. "Don't be usin' that word! It's not for you!"

"Shit, I'm 'bout to spark this weed, goddamn," Rosie replied, producing a six-inch rolled blunt from the center pocket of her hoodie.

She pulled a lighter from the pocket of her baggy jeans and lit the huge, homemade Marijuana cigar.

A cloud of smoke filled the front room of the trailer.

Rosie's mom, Shelly, strolled in through the haze like a tired and haggard white trash rock star trying to strut through stage fog. Rosie passed her the blunt.

Shelly took a long hit and handed it back, then exhaled all over Keety Boy, who remained hunched over the Shorty Trickum Christmas commemorative plate on the coffee table in front of the couch that covered the hole in the floor where the goblins crept in at night when no one was paying attention. Shelly drew a bead on the couch. Her memory fluttered back into childhood. The trailer's interior squiggly and blurred as Shelly fell into the time warp and then she was seven years old.

Pawpaw had told Shelly about the goblins, about how they were the ones that touched her little girl's places while she was asleep, her head heavy with medicine, too heavy to stir. It was the goblins who couldn't resist her, she was just too pretty.

Shelly frowned and shook off the memory. *It was the goblins...*

"Yo, nigga, where Pawpaw at?" she asked Keety Boy.

He cringed again and gripped the pink straw tight. Squeezing his eyes shut, Keety exclaimed, "Goddammit stop saying that word! Y'all are white trash trailer kids! That word ain't for y'all! Just look at 'cha with your pale skin, freckles, wily curls, and dull eyes!"

Rosie and Shelly laughed and shared an incredulous look.

"Damn, yo, you sound like you describing characters in a story or some shit," Rosie said. Suddenly, her brow creased and she mumbled, "Fuck shit; what if we in a story?"

Shelly laughed at Rosie's musings, then turned back to KeetyBoy. "Where Pawpaw at?" She asked again.

Keety Boy exhaled hard and shouted for his grandfather.

A knocking echoed from across the room, followed by the jiggling of a handle.

Thirteen seconds later the pudgy little man fell out of the living room closet, clad only in stained briefs and a trucker hat. He scratched his balls and sneezed. Shelly ran to him.

"Pawpaw, I need some money. You got some money?"

The man arched an eyebrow and made a lewd sexual gesture with his hands.

Shelly rolled her eyes and bit her bottom lip. Pawpaw rubbed his thumb and forefingers together, the universal sign for cash money, then bounced his bushy black eyebrows.

"Fine, okay," Shelly said, her voice filled with exasperation.

Pawpaw tilted on his toes, smiled wildly, and twiddled his fingers.

Shelly started toward the master bedroom. "C'mon on, then," she said.

Pawpaw followed and shut the door behind them.

Keety Boy shook his head in disapproval, then finally snorted the rail of meth he'd cut out.

His eyes bolted wide. He shouted, "Oh my Gawd, it's almost Christmas! I gotta get presents!"

Sinking into the couch amid a haze of smoke, Rosie murmured, "How you gonna buy presents? You a broke ass nigga."

"I told you, stop saying that—"

"Yo!" Rosie hollered, cutting Keety off, "You should sell that meth shit to get Christmas money, dawg."

A celestial chorus of bells sounded off in Keety Boy's head, obscuring the grunts and moans and sighing of bed springs that echoed from the master bedroom. He leapt off the floor.

"I got it! I'll sell meth to get money for Christmas presents!"

"Yo, that's what I just said, ni–"

"And I'll use a magical meth recipe from Mawmaw's *Christmas Cauldron* Cookbook, just like she telled me to!"

"Yo, she don't let nobody use that book. You can't—"

"And it'll be the bestest Christmas of all times!"

Rosie started to warn Keety Boy of the reported dangers of Mawmaw's fabled holiday cookbook but instead she sighed with resignation, offered a grin, and said softly, "Yeah, KB, the best of all time."

A moment of peaceful silence passed between Rosie and Keety Boy before the bedroom door swung open. Shelly limped out with one hand clutching her back side and a fat wad of cash in the other.

"Got-Damn, Pawpaw done rurnt my asshole!" Shelly proclaimed. "Let's get the shit up outta this bitch."

Rosie peeled herself off the couch, saying, "Yo KB, we be back for Christmas Eve dinner."

"When's that?" Keety Boy asked.

"It's tomorrow, nigga," Rosie shouted, throwing a made-up gang sign.

Keety Boy's face turned blood red. "I told you, stop–"

"Yo, we out!" Shelly hollered as she and Rosie tumbled out the front door and into the frosty morning air before Keety Boy could admonish them any further on his beliefs regarding cultural appropriation.

Keety Boy gazed out the window at the gray sky, then checked the clock on the ancient VCR. 8:08 a.m. He needed to get to work. But what was it he was going to do?

He was standing at the window, staring at the sky and trying to remember when Mawmaw appeared with Pawpaw in tow, who was dressed in flannel and jeans, matching with Mawmaw. They both sported festive Santa hats.

As they pulled on heavy winter coats, Mawmaw said, "Listen here, Keety, we going to play the numbers and the ding-dings. You remember what I said and stay outta ma *Christmas Cauldron* Cookbook, ya hear."

Keety Boy's eyes lit up. He rolled his jaw and stretched his neck.

"You hear me, boy?" Mawmaw said.

"Yes ma'am, I hear ya!" Keety replied.

"Good, then. We be back in a few hours. You stay good."

"Yes ma'am."

Keety Boy smiled wide and watched his grandparents drive away in Li'l Big'un, Mawmaw's monster truck. Thanks to Mawmaw, he remembered his mission: to cook the greatest, most magical meth that he could and make this the bestest, most wonderousest, gawdamned awesoemestest Christmas of all time, ever!! Keety gazed at the gray sky and his heart filled with the magic and joy of Christmas, and as tears of happiness pooled in his eyes, thick flakes of snow began to fall.

"It's snowing! It's Christmas magic!" Keety Boy screeched.

And the wonder of the season filled his heart. He threw on his shoes and dashed out to the lab. It was time to get to work. There was no time to waste, for Christmas waits for no one, especially those who have no time to wait.

LOCKED AWAY IN THE shed out behind the trailer, like a junior high chemistry student with dreams of one day becoming a full-time mad scientist, Keety Boy surveyed his meth lab. All the ingredients were in place. Mawmaw's Cookbook lay opened on the table, turned to the family recipe for gingerbread meth. He went back over the list one last time just to make sure it was all there.

"Let's see," he said to himself. "Cinnamon, ginger, cloves, uh, powdered fingernail clippings from town shaman, evaporated dreams of middle-aged husbands, freeze-dried orphan nightmares, pinch of dried and powdered jizz of senior level demon, organic powdered breast milk of pregnant rape victim." He scanned through the cook book one very, absolutely, totally, for real last time, in hopes of calming his raging, overjoyed nerves. His eyes trembled. He licked his dry lips. It was all there. "Good thing Mawmaw had all them fixins in her secret witch's cupboard!"

And so, he began.

Tirelessly, Keety Boy cooked all day and into the night until, at the break of dawn on Christmas Eve, his task was complete. It was time to share the wonder of his creation, and make some money so he could buy presents too.

And snow continued to fall on Mable Town.

CHRISTMAS
Motherfucking Eve
(Goddamn!)

DUSK

Trudging through the snow, Keety Boy tripped over a headless baby doll that had been buried in the front yard to bring good luck. He never understood how it was that John, Paul, and Mary had created their own form of voodoo. Why couldn't they just believe in Jesus like everyone else? As Keety neared the trailer's front door, moans of pleasure and whoops of excitement and joy tickled his ears.

"Oh lord, what'r they up to now?" Keety muttered to himself.

Unable to quell his curiosity, Keety peeked through the wide, unadorned picture window (the window which any old person, any old time, could see right the fuck into), and immediately regretted the decision.

There on the living room floor were John, Paul, and Mary, making an Eiffel Tower.

"Oh my, good lord!" Keety Boy said to himself, quickly turning away.

Not wanting to disturb their amorous activities, Keety pulled his winter parka close, tightened the hood over his head, and waited for his neighbors to finish. To Keety's chagrin, the three lovers had hired a professional Sexy Time Commentator who was relating all the action in loud, colorful language.

Suddenly, they cut to a commercial break! (Oh, my fucking gawd, y'all!)

Looking to spice up your love life? Tired of the same old quiet, intimate love making? Then it's time to bring in a Valkos brand Sexy Time Commentator!

Valkos brand Sexy Time Commentators help you make the most of those special times, describing your every move back to you in stunning, erotic detail! Using the most advanced vocal techniques and language, your personal Commentator can turn a drab encounter into an explosive, unforgettable experience, helping you and your partner or partners reach orgasmic heights you'd never dreamed of.

Order your Valkos brand Sexy Time Commentator today, and let your passion be enunciated like never before!

And now back to our regularly scheduled, bitch-ass programming!

Keety Boy was suddenly struck by the memory of the time Pawpaw had hired a Sexy Time Commentator for Shelly's fifteenth birthday. Pawpaw and eight of his coworkers from the Odle Griesiends salad factory had run a train on her, each taking their turn abusing her young, fragile flesh, and then doing it again, then again, and then one more time just because they could, and also because Titanium Dick Erectors for Men (Goddammit! Edition) lasted a really long fucking time. Shelly hadn't been able to walk for a week after that, and she wept every time she peed or thought of Vienna Sausages.

Assaulted by the memory, Keety spun left and puked up a torrent of pink bile. He shook his head and wiped his mouth with the sleeve of his parka. As the vomit seeped into the snow, Keety sniffled and tears slipped out of his eyes.

"C'mon now, no tears," he whispered to himself, his own voice eclipsed by the commentary and shouting coming from the trailer. "It's Christmas. Happy thoughts, happy thoughts..."

The voices in the trailer rose in volume.

"And it looks like they're coming in for a big finish, folks!" The commentator hollered through his portable microphone and amplification system. "John is really pounding Mary's pussy now, while Mary is sucking Paul's cock for dear life. Yes, yes, oh yeah baby it's about that time. They're going, and they're going, and theeeeeyyyyy'rrrreeee— gone!!"

John, Paul, and Mary simultaneously erupted in an explosive climax.

The commentator shouted, "Incredible! That may have been the sexiest sex that this humble commentator has ever seen!" as the three entwined partners collapsed on the floor.

"What a finish, ladies and gentlemen, what a gorgeous finish. We have seen true glory here tonight, folks!" The commentator said in conclusion.

DOORBUSTERS 63

Keety Boy felt his own dick shrinking as he shivered in the cold. After a couple of minutes had passed, he decided he couldn't wait any longer. He gave the door a hefty knock and hoped that whoever answered would be at least somewhat clothed.

The door was opened by a short, busty woman whose thin robe could barely contain her voluptuous assets. She smiled. "Hey there Keety Boy! What chu doin' out here in this weather? Get on in here and warm yourself up!"

Keety thanked Mary and scooted into the trailer, shaking snow off his back.

"It's really comin' down out there. I ain't never seen the likes 'a this," Keety Boy said. Noticing John and Paul sprawled out on the couch, also wearing tattered house coats, he waved meekly and said hello. As Keety greeted his neighbors, the Sexy Time Commentator slipped out quietly, offering a "Merry Christmas to you all" just before stepping out the door.

"What's goin' on with you?" John asked.

Once the professional commentator was out of earshot, Keety said in a blur, "John, I got the best goddamn Christmas meth you ever had you won't believe it you gotta try it I'm lettin' it go for a real good price too yeah I'm sellin' to buy Christmas presents for ever'one!"

"Christmas meth?" John said. "Oh hell, gimme somma that shit!"

Keety Boy produced a baggie full of the gingerbread brown drugs and passed it to John, who excitedly inspected it. Paul and Mary joined in and each bought a bag of their own. As Keety pocketed the cash, his three neighbors cut out long rails of drugs on the dirty glass top of the coffee table.

Noticing the amount of the gingerbread meth cut out on the table, Keety Boy said, "Um, y'all don't really need that much. This here shit is strong, and 'sides, it's got enchantments, too."

Mary, John, and Paul snickered.

"It's got what, now?" Mary said.

"Enchantments," Keety Boy answered. "You know...magic."

The three neighbors shook their heads and giggled.

"KB, you crack me up, son," Paul said as he pulled a short, dirty white straw from the pocket of his robe.

"Y'all, I think what Keety is sayin' is that it's made with love. It'n that right, Keety Boy?" Mary added.

Knowing that they would never believe him if he were to explain to them that the gingerbread meth was in fact a crystalized magic potion, he simply nodded and said, "Yeah, uh, that's right, Mary."

"Hey, you gone have some with us?" John asked.

Keety shook his head. "Naw, y'all go ahead."

"C'mon, now," John said.

"I already had some earlier this morning," Keety Boy lied, feeling the fear inside that he had for his own creation. He'd snorted a small line of the regular meth that he had left over, just enough to keep him going.

"Well, have some more, it's Christmas," Paul added.

"Yeah, KB, it's Christmas," Mary said, smiling wide. "Just stay a while; just do a little."

Keety Boy smiled nervously and said, "Oh all right, guess I got time to visit for a bit."

"Hell yeah, now, get in here," John said while the three scooched over and made a place at the coffee table for their friend.

Keety pulled out another small bag of gingerbread meth and chopped out a line for himself. After a bit of chiding from Paul and John, Keety Boy's line turned into a rail.

"Merry Christmas!" John said.

"Merry Christmas!" Keety, Mary, and Paul replied.

And as if bowing in prayer, they all bent low and snorted their destinies up their noses.

MARY FELL BACKWARDS onto the dirty carpet. She writhed on her back and said, "Oh lord, Keety, that is sooooooo gooooood! It's so good, oh God it's so, so good!"

Like a happy cat, Mary rolled back and forth on her back, proclaiming the glory of Keety Boy's creation.

John eyed her curiously. His features twitched. "I think she's blowin' up," he said.

"What's that, now?" Paul asked.

"Look at 'er." John pointed. "I swear her feet 'r puffin' up."

Paul looked at Mary. In that instant, she rolled out of her robe and squirmed naked on the filthy carpet floor. Her huge breasts flopped over her chest and rested in her armpits as she raised her hands above her head and stretched.

Keety Boy looked away but Paul and John remained fixated.

Mary grabbed her left breast and massaged the nipple. She cooed and slipped her fingers deep into her vagina. While gyrating and moaning and pleasuring herself, Mary's whole body began to grow.

As she inflated, she moaned louder and louder, her voice booming and filling the trailer. Her skin stretched and began to tear.

"Oh, my Gawd, KB, what'd you give 'er?? What's in that shit??" John shouted.

"I told y'all, it's magic Christmas meth!" Keety Boy shouted back.

Paul hopped up off the floor and backed away from his ever-expanding second cousin. He screamed, "She's gonna blow! Mary's gonna pop!"

Mary's self-love intensified and her voice still raised higher and higher, louder and louder.

Wide-eyed, Keety Boy scrambled, shoving all the baggies of meth back into his satchel. Grabbing his coat, he ran for the door. "Merry Christmas, y'all!" He hollered as he stumbled out the front door.

As soon as Keety Boy slammed the trailer's front door behind him, an explosion blew the door out of its frame, slamming Keety in the back and sending him hurtling face first into the snow. Through the ringing in his ears, KB could hear John Shrinking, "She dun blowed up! Mary blowed the fuck up!"

"Keety Boy!" Paul screamed, "Look what you dun you sum-bitchin' bastard! We gonna git you, boy, we gonna git yuuuuu..."

Paul's last word trailed off into a guttural growl which was quickly followed by more growls, animalistic grunts, and pained half-humanoid screams.

Keety Boy whimpered, "Aw shit, that don't sound good." He army-crawled out from under the door.

The sweet stench of scorched flesh wafted out of the trailer. The walls and furniture were soaked with blood, entrails, and bits of Mary.

A swirling ball of blazing yellow light floated in the center of the trailer's main room, illuminating the gore with a serene, warm glow. Beneath the sphere of light were John and Paul, hunched over...changing.

"Oh lord, that ain't good a 'tall!" Keety Boy shouted to himself. And without a further thought, he turned and ran.

WHEN KEETY BOY BURST in through the front door of the trailer that he shared with Mawmaw and Pawpaw, the grandparents were already gathered around the kitchen table, snorting the lines of gingerbread meth that Keety Boy had carelessly left out, and passing around a bowl of green bean casserole.

"Don't! Put that shit down, it ain't no good!" Keety cried as he ran toward the table.

"What 'chu talking about, Nigga, this shit is fire!" Rosie exclaimed.

Keety Boy was so wigged out he didn't even have time to cringe at her dumb ass.

"I would be mad at 'cha, 'cept for but this here holiday meth is so good," Mawmaw said. "I'm 'bout to have a second rail!"

Pawpaw giggled and clapped his hands before puking beside the table and snorting another huge line of meth.

"You done good, Keety Boy, real good. I'm mighty proud of ya," Mawmaw said.

"Yeah, KB, this here shit is the shit, for reals, yo!" Shelly added.

Keety Boy smiled bashfully and batted his eyes. "Y'all really think so?"

Everyone at the table nodded enthusiastically in the affirmative.

Keety said, "Aw, shucks, y'all, I feel like I could cry I'm so hap—"

He was abruptly cut off by Pawpaw spewing a torrent of blood-filled vomit onto the table, soaking the turkey and the stuffing and all the fixins.

Mawmaw screamed. Shelly and Rosie took out their phones and started filming.

Pawpaw's skin took on a gelatinous glow. His body quivered. Blood and foam poured from the corners of his mouth. The top of his skull split open.

The bulbous head of an erect penis the size of Pawpaw's skull rose out of his ruined head. His face slid off and his skin collapsed. His body fell away and in its place was a huge, throbbing cock with tiny, T-Rex like arms that sported three claws at the end of each appendage.

Giant dick Pawpaw bounced two times and unleashed a torrent of thick, pale yellow jizz onto Shelly.

"Gawd, no!" Shelly howled. "It's my quinceañera all over again!"

Shelly's skin bubbled and burned, releasing a sick, sweet aroma. She cried out in agony as monster Pawpaw's man sauce ate through her flesh. Blood-encrusted, used tampons grew out of every hole that the acidic jizz burrowed through her body. Shelly's screams morphed into watery wails. Her Christmas sweater disintegrated under the cleansing power of the jizz to expose a dark, red line from her collar bone to her navel. The red line thickened. Shelly's body shook. The red line split wide, pulling her chest apart. An enormous vagina grew out of Shelly's chest, severing her head, pushing off her breasts and torso until Shelly had become a giant vagina with spindly arms and legs.

The vagina monster roared with anger and dove onto the Pawpaw dick atrocity, swallowing it whole. Obnoxious chewing noises echoed from the 'gina while its lips flapped furiously. The chewing stopped abruptly and the Shelly monster spewed a river of blood and masticated flesh all over Rosie, who was smoking a blunt and filming on her phone.

Rosie screeched and hollered and wailed and cried and cussed and whined and alluded and alliterated as the putrid mess covered her.

Objects started growing out of Rosie's flesh. Tainted aluminum foil grew on her arms. Crumpled paper popped up on her hands. Her feet turned into carry out boxes.

Rosie screamed, "Yo, nigga, I'm turnin' into a pile of garbage! That meth was bunk! I'm a kill yo ass, KB!"

Keety Boy ran to the family weapons display case in the living room and grabbed the chainsaw that sat on the top shelf of the cabinet, glowing in the radiance of a bare forty-watt light bulb, gassed up and ready to go, just like always.

"Come on, Bessie, time to do some work," Keety Boy said as he grabbed the saw off the shelf.

He flipped off the safety, yanked the cord, and Bessie the badass chainsaw roared to life.

Shelly the vagina monster wheezed, "You stupid worm, you ain't gonna hurt us! You can't do nothin' 'cept fuck up. You a dumb bastard, that's what you are, just stupid fuckin' stupid, and that's all you'll ever be."

The words cut Keety to the quick. There it was again, the one that hurt the most: *Stupid.*

That's what they called him in school before he dropped out. It's what his siblings called him at home. *Stupid; fucking stupid.*

Tears filled Keety Boy's eyes, blurring his vision. But they weren't tears of sadness, they were tears of rage. All of the pain he'd kept pushed deep down inside rose to the surface. And he was ready. Keety let the power of the sorrow and anger fill and consume him.

And the enchanted meth worked its magic.

Tears flowed down his cheeks. Keety Boy revved the machine to full-tilt-boogie and lunged at Shelly with Bessie leading the way.

Before Shelly could react, Keety plunged the saw blade deep into the bottom of the vagina monster. He pulled upward, cutting through the soft flesh, screaming as blood and viscera rained down on him.

The saw tore through the top of the creature and the two halves hopped away on one leg and collapsed dead on the floor.

Rosie the garbage monster stomped toward Keety Boy, screaming, "Yo, nigga, you killed Shelly! I'm 'bout to fuck yo ass up!"

Keety Boy revved the saw. At the top of his lungs he shouted with vehemence, "I told you; stop saying that "N" Word!!"

Rosie swung a hard left. Keety met her arm with the saw and lopped it off. Dark green garbage juice spewed from the wound. Undeterred, Rosie landed a right hook on Keety, knocking him over the table. The spinning saw blade fell onto his left leg as he hit the floor, the blade digging into his soft flesh.

Keety howled and snatched the saw off his leg.

Rosie leapt over the table. Just as she was coming down on Keety, he swung the saw up, cutting off Rosie's garbage legs at the knees, and rolling out of the way just before she landed.

As she writhed on the floor beside him, putrid garbage slime shot out of Rosie's leg stumps, splashing on Keety Boy's chest.

"My Christmas sweater!" He shouted.

In a fit of fury, Keety rammed the chainsaw up into Rosie and sawed her in half from her gentle folds to the top of her head where her mother kissed her and smelled her hair when Rosie was just a tiny babe.

....

Don't miss out!

Visit the website below and you can sign up to receive emails whenever Russell Holbrook publishes a new book. There's no charge and no obligation.

https://books2read.com/r/B-A-RUSI-BJEDF

BOOKS 2 READ

Connecting independent readers to independent writers.

Did you love *Doorbusters*? Then you should read *Lucy Furr*[1] by Russell Holbrook!

SOMETIMES IT TAKES A DEVIL TO DO THE LORD'S WORK Mable Town has come under the rule of the oppressive Valkos Enterprises government, forcing their brand on the populous and demanding conformity with every aspect of its citizens' lives. Even so, Mary, Joseph, and their cat, Lucy Furr, are happy with their mundane existence. That is until a malicious group of teenagers attack the beloved feline, causing a gruesome and deadly chain of events. Lucy Furr is a surreal, gore-soaked thrill-ride for both horror and dark fantasy fiction fans alike!

---

1. https://books2read.com/u/megZJE

2. https://books2read.com/u/megZJE

Also by Russell Holbrook

Heroin is the Answer: A Memoir of What I Can Remember
Lucy Furr
The Distended Table: A Collection of Holiday Favorites
Wanda the Bloodtose Intolerant Vampire
Piper and Shelly and the Weird Thing That Happened
Cärl Brüder Versus the Self-Publishing Apocalypse!
Ever a Never After
I'm Only With You Because I am Afraid to be Alone
Doorbusters

About the Author

Staff writer #001428, Russell Holbrook, writes books, stories, and music exclusively for the glory of Valkos Enterprises' Department of Letters and Distractionary Materials. He has been a faithful and steadfast employee of the division since 1989 when, as a teenager, he was moved from his assignment on the conveyor line at the Valkos computer parts recycling supercenter to the Writers of Distractionary Materials warehouse where he continues to occupy his very own desk with an inspirational cactus, under a small window on the 17th floor. He lives in West Mable Town with his legally registered life partner and their five furry children.

About the Publisher

Established in 2017 by Svaden Von Valkos III, Splatterpiece Press is a boutique publisher specializing in the bizarre and macabre. It operates under the Valkos Enterprises Department of Letters and Distractionary Materials, a branch of the Valkos Enterprises Division of Entertainment and Programming Propaganda. Having left his job as a lead dishwasher at Fun n' Games Family Fun Center, Svaden reluctantly joined the family business after being promised the opportunity to run his very own division over which he would have complete and total creative control. With a small team and grand ambitions, he began releasing their dark creations into the world.